The stories at this level

These stories are still centred round the pe
your child has the fun and security of meetiⁿg ⁻⁻
These characters are also shown reading their own favourite books wiⁿⁿ
their parents. The West Street 'children' like reading fairy stories, rhymes
and legends. This emphasises how much all children enjoy reading and
sharing stories with their parents, and how much this is a normal part of
everyday life. It will also encourage your children to share their own
enjoyment of the characters coming to life in these stories.

Before you start reading the book with your child, read the story and
activities first yourself, so that you become familiar with the text and the
best way to give it expression and emphasis when reading it aloud.

Always sit comfortably with your child, so that both of you can see the
book easily. Read the story, making it sound as interesting as possible.
Encourage your child to participate actively in the reading, to turn over the
pages and to become involved in the story and characters. You may find
that your child is ready to share in the reading more quickly than before.

Sometimes let your children look through the book before you start
reading, and for a change, let them guess what the story is about from the
pictures. Encourage them to talk about the pictures, and add your own
suggestions, if you wish, to help them with the story line.

This may be enough for one sitting, but don't give your child the idea that
the book is finished with. Encourage your child to take the book away and
to look through it alone, to find any bits that either of you particularly
enjoyed.

Next time you look at the book with your child, suggest "Let's read the
story together. You join in with me. If you want to go on reading on your
own, give my arm a little push (or any other signal you prefer), and I'll stop
reading and you go on. Give me another push when you want me to join
in with you again." Let your child follow the words with a finger *under*
them. Don't stop to repeat or correct words: keep the interest up and the
story flowing along.

The next time you both look at the book, have a quick chat about the contents of the story, then invite your child to read it to you without you reading as well. Give help with words or phrases that cause difficulty. Join in with the reading again if your child is struggling with the story.

The activities at this level

The activities at the back of the book need not be completed at once. They are not a test, but will help your child to remember the words and stories and to develop further the skills required for becoming a fluent reader.

The activities are often divided into three parts:

One part is designed to encourage you both to talk about the stories, and to link them where possible with your child's own experiences. Encourage your child to predict what will happen and to recall the main events of the story. Change the wording of the story as much as you like and encourage your children to tell you about the story in their own way.

One part encourages children to look back through the book to find general or specific things in the text or the pictures. Your child learns to begin to look at the text itself, and to recognise individual words and letters more precisely. The activities state clearly when you should give a letter its name, and when you should sound it out. The activities also introduce more writing, largely copying from words in the original story. If your children find this too difficult, copy the words onto a piece of paper for them to trace over.

One part includes activities which your child can do without your help. It may be necessary, though, to read the instructions to your child, pointing out the words as you do so. Read the instructions to the *first* activity only in this way. Then say "Would you like to try this on your own?" One activity at a time is probably enough for your child to do in one sitting.

When all the activities have been done, encourage your child to read the story again before you move on to another book. Your child should now feel secure with it and enjoy reading to you.

The hare and the tortoise

by Helen Arnold

Illustrated by Val Biro and Tony Kenyon

A Piccolo Original
In association with Macmillan Education

Will you read us a story, Dad?
What kind of story?

4

A story about some animals.
A story about a race.

5

I'll read you a story about
a hare and a tortoise.
Oh good! I like that story.

Once upon a time there was a hare and a tortoise.

Tortoise sat in the sun.
It made him sleepy.

Hare jumped over Tortoise and
ran round and round him.

Then Hare had an idea.

"Would you like some nice
cabbages?" said Hare.
Tortoise grunted.

"I'll race you to the cabbage
patch," said Hare.
Tortoise grunted again.

So Hare and Tortoise got ready
to race to the cabbage patch.

Hare ran very fast, but Tortoise went
slowly down the path.

It was very hot in the sun.
Soon Hare began to feel thirsty.

"I'll stop for a little drink,"
said Hare.

So Hare had a little drink and
Tortoise went on down the path
to the cabbage patch.

Hare ran on down the path.

It was very hot in the sun.
Soon Hare began to feel tired.

"I'll stop for a little sleep,"
said Hare.
"Tortoise can't catch me."

So Hare fell fast asleep and
Tortoise went on down the path
to the cabbage patch.

Tortoise saw Hare was fast asleep.
He went on down the path
to the cabbage patch.

"What nice cabbages,"
said Tortoise.
"I feel hungry after that race."
So Tortoise began to eat
the cabbages.

The sun went down and
Hare woke up.

"Tortoise can't catch me," said Hare
and he ran on down the path to
the cabbage patch.

"Where are all the cabbages?"
said Hare.
"Inside me!" said Tortoise.

26

So Tortoise ate all the cabbages.
And he won the race!

27

Things to talk about with your children

1. Why didn't Hare win the race?
  Who do you like most, Hare or Tortoise? Why?

Do you remember any other stories about animals?
Tell me one that you liked.

2. Which of these things really happened in the story?
Which did not happen?
  Hare jumped over Tortoise.
  Hare began to eat the cabbages.
  Tortoise had a little sleep.
  Hare had a little drink.

3. Which of these animals run very fast?
Which of these animals are very slow?

Draw a picture of a slow animal and write slow under it.

Draw a picture of a fast animal and write fast under it.

Looking at pictures and words
with your children

1. Can you read these bits from the story to me?

can't catch me   fast asleep

he won the race

began to feel thirsty

Now draw a picture of Hare and a picture of Tortoise.

Which of the words you have read belong to Hare?
Write them under Hare's picture.

Which of the words you have read belong to Tortoise?
Write them under Tortoise's picture.

2. Copy out all the words in the story that end in y.

Can you read them to me?

Things for your child to do

plane

baby

tricycle

car

speed boat

rowing boat

tractor

Draw all the **fast** things in the picture.

Now draw all the **slow** things.

Now you can write the names of the things under each of your pictures, if you like.

These activities and skills:	will help your children to:
Looking and remembering	hold a story in their heads, retell it in their own words.
Listening, being able to tell the difference between sounds	remember sounds in words and link spoken words with the words they see in print.
Naming things and using different words to explain or retell events	recognise different words in print, build their vocabulary and guess at the meaning of words.
Matching, seeing patterns, similarities and differences	recognise letters, see patterns within words, use the patterns to read 'new' words and split long words into syllables.
Knowing the grammatical patterns of spoken language	guess the word-order in reading.
Anticipating what is likely to happen next in a story	guess what the next sentence or event is likely to be about.
Colouring, getting control of pencils and pens, copying and spelling	produce their own writing, which will help them to understand the way English is written.
Understanding new experiences by linking them to what they already know	read with understanding and think about what they have read.
Understanding their own feelings and those of others	enjoy and respond to stories and identify with the characters.

First published 1989 by Pan Books Ltd, Cavaye Place, London SW10 9PG

9 8 7 6 5 4 3 2 1

Editorial consultant: Donna Bailey

© Pan Books Ltd and Macmillan Publishers Ltd 1989. Text © Helen Arnold 1989

British Library Cataloguing in Publication Data
Arnold, Helen
The hare and the tortoise.
1. English language. Readers – For children
I. Title   II. Series
428.6
ISBN 0–330–30222–1

Printed in Hong Kong